Sam looked in Sid's box,
He looked behind some sticks
and leaves.
"He is gone," said Sam.

Sid was the school's pet snake.
All the children loved Sid.

"We have to look for him!"
said Maya.
"He is hiding from us."

The door opened, and in walked
Mrs Hill with a new teacher.

Mrs Hill

"Come in," said Mrs Hill
to the new teacher.
"This is Maya and Sam.
They help to look
after the school animals."

"We have lots of animals,"
said Mrs Hill.
"We have rabbits and mice,
AND we have a pet snake!"

"Oh, dear!" said the new teacher.
"I don't like snakes at all!"

Bang!

Sam and Maya looked up.
They saw an animal moving
along the bookshelf.
It was long and brown.
It was moving very slowly.

The new teacher looked up, too.

"**_Eeeeeeeeekkkkkkkk!_**" he cried.

"It's a snake!"

He ran out the door
and hid behind a big tree.

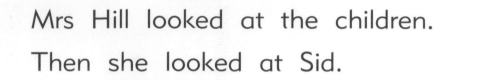

Mrs Hill looked at the children.
Then she looked at Sid.

"Sid got out of his box,"
said Maya.
"We were looking for him."

"But," smiled Sam,
"Sid was hiding from us!"